Rainbow House

Vivian French

Illustrated by Biz Hull

Tamarind Ltd

Sponsored by NASUWT

Diandra loved Mondays.
On Mondays she walked
the long way home from school with her Mum,
the way that went past Rainbow House.

Diandra knew that Rainbow House was the most wonderful house in town. It was big, with a huge rainbow painted on the wall, and every room had different coloured curtains.

It was full of people, but they didn't hurry about like Mum always did. They sat very still, or walked very slowly. Diandra liked that.

"Can't we go this way every day?"
Diandra asked Mum.

"I wish we could," said Mum,
"but I have work to do."
Diandra sighed.
Mum always had work to do.

When the weather grew warm and sunny,
the windows of Rainbow House sprang open.

Diandra tugged at Mum's arm as they walked by.
"Look, Mum, look!" she said.

The red and orange, yellow and pink, blue, green
and violet curtains fluttered and danced in the wind.

"Come along, Diandra," Mum said.

Diandra made up stories about Rainbow House.

"Did you see the man looking out of the blue room?"
she asked. "Well, he looks after the sky.
When the weather is grey he gets his broom
and he sweeps away the clouds."

"Oh, Diandra!" Mum said, but she was smiling.

The next week Diandra
saw a woman
behind the red curtains.

"Look, Mum!" she said.
"That woman takes care of all
the cherries and berries in the world.
When they're green and hard she blows very, very softly…
and ABRACADABRA!!
They turn red and sweet and juicy."

Mum stopped for a moment to look.

"Fancy that!" she said.

The week after that, someone waved to Diandra
from behind the green curtains.

"Oh!" said Diandra, "Oh! Did you see?
He waved at me!"

Mum laughed. "And does he have a story, Diandra?"

Diandra gave a little skip.

"Perhaps he tip-toes
out at night,
touching the trees
with his fingers…
and the leaves
grow green
and beautiful."

Two weeks later Diandra saw the notice.

It was pinned to the curly iron gates, and Diandra knew it was special because there was a rainbow at the top.

"What does it say?" she asked Mum.

OPEN DAY
COME AND SEE WHO WE
ARE AND WHAT WE DO
TEA BISCUITS AND A
WARM WELCOME
SATURDAY 12 to 5

Diandra could hardly speak.

"Mum!" breathed Diandra. "Mum! Does that mean we can really, really go in?"

Mum nodded, "That's right."

"Will we see the blue room and the red room and all the rooms?"

Mum suddenly stopped.
"Oh, Diandra!" she said.
"I don't think we can come
on Saturday."

Diandra stared at Mum.
"But we must!" she said.

Mum took Diandra's hand,
and led her to a bench nearby.

"Diandra," she said, "Rainbow House isn't what you think.
It's not anywhere magic! It's just a home for very old people.
Some are ill. They have nurses to look after them."

Diandra shook her head. "I still want to go," she said.
"I know it's magic. You'll see!"

Mum sighed. "Well... I suppose I can find the time.
We can't stay long though!"

When Saturday came Diandra was up very early.

"Mum! Mum! Where are my green hair ribbons?
Where's my red skirt?
Where are my pink socks?"

"Diandra," said Mum, "I've had a hard week.
Rainbow House doesn't open until twelve o'clock.
Let's have some peace and quiet!"

Diandra crept away and dressed.
She looked at herself and then she took off
one pink sock and put on an orange one instead.

At last Mum came to help her.

"I've put out the ribbons," said Diandra.
"Green ones! I'm a rainbow girl today!"

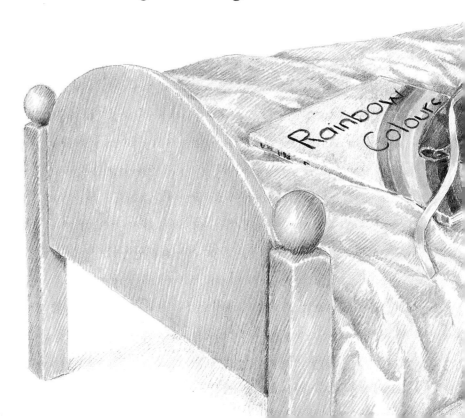

Mum looked at Diandra and smiled.
"You certainly are," she said.

Finally it was twelve o'clock.

"Can we go? Can we go now?" Diandra begged,
and she picked up her school bag.
It was very full.

"What have you got in there,
Diandra?" Mum asked.

"A book and a puzzle.
They're presents
for the rainbow people."

"Diandra," Mum said,
"the people in Rainbow House
are very, very old.
They may not want your books."

Diandra held on to her bag.
"They will, you'll see,"
she said.

Diandra and Mum walked through the gates
and up the drive.

Together they went through the front door
and into the house.

"Oh!" said Diandra. And she stared.

The room was large and airy,
and full of chairs. A big television set
was making a lot of noise in one corner.

A nurse in a white uniform came bustling over.

"Good afternoon," she said. "How nice of you to come.
Would you like a cup of tea?"

"Thank you," Mum said and she sat down.

"Would your little girl like some juice?" asked the nurse.

"No, thank you," said Diandra.

She took the book
out of her bag and
walked straight over
to two old women
sitting at a table.

"Hello," she said. "I'm Diandra."

"That's a pretty name, dear," said one of the women. "I'm Violet. And this is Rose."

"Oh!" Diandra's face lit up like sunshine. "You've even got rainbow names! I told Mum this was a magic place!"

A man sitting nearby growled.
"Magic?" he said crossly. "No magic here. Silly child."

"Hush, Clyde," Rose said quickly. "And what's this book you've brought, dear?"

"It's a present!" Diandra said. "Look! I'll show you!"

Clyde scowled. "Book? Book? How can we read books? Print's too small!"
And he turned his back on Diandra.

"It's my favourite," Diandra told Rose,
"but I want you to have it
because it's about rainbows
and colours."

Violet suddenly
leant forward.

"Goodness gracious!"
she exclaimed.

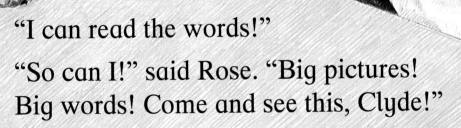

"I can read the words!"

"So can I!" said Rose. "Big pictures!
Big words! Come and see this, Clyde!"

"No," said Clyde.

Diandra went over to Clyde. She dug in her bag.
"I've got a jigsaw for you."

Clyde didn't look at the jigsaw. He held out his hand instead.
"See that?" he said.

Diandra saw that his fingers were all swollen.

"How can I do jigsaws?"

Diandra smiled her hugest smile. "But Mr Clyde!"
she said, "you can, look!"

This time Clyde looked. Diandra was spreading the jigsaw over the table. They were big, big pieces.

"Ah," Clyde said, and very carefully he picked up one piece and slowly fitted it into another. "Ah."

"There!" Diandra said happily.
"It's a good jigsaw, isn't it, Mr Clyde?"

Clyde nodded, and put another piece in place.
"You've got sense," he said.
"But I'm Mr Green. Not Mr Clyde."

Diandra bounced her way back to Mum.

"Mum, Mum! I was right!
There's a Rose and a Violet and a Mr Green!
And they love my book and the jigsaw! LOOK!"

Rose was reading.
Clyde was doing the jigsaw.
No-one was watching the television any more.
They were all trying to see what was going on.

Violet stroked Diandra's head.

"Such beautiful corn-rows," she said, and touched Diandra's hair. "I used to have hair like yours."

"Mum did it!" Diandra said. "She can do anything with hair. She'll do your hair too, if you like. But she does tweak it a bit."

Violet laughed. "I don't mind tweaking," she said. "My own mum was a terrible tweaker!"

She gave Mum a little smile. "I don't suppose you'd have time. We've seen you walking past. You seem to be a very busy woman..."

"Well..." she said "I suppose
I could call in on a Monday."

"Thank you!" said Diandra,
and she beamed at Mum.

"Thank you!" said Violet.

"In fact," Mum said slowly,
"I could come every Monday.
I'd have to bring Diandra too...
but I don't think she'd mind that!"

"Diandra," asked Mum, as they were leaving, "weren't you sad not to see the sky man and the berry lady?"

"But I did!" said Diandra. "They were ALL there!"

"Were they?" asked Mum, surprised. "Are you sure?"

Diandra sighed. "Of course they were," she said.
"But they have to look like ordinary people on the outside.
Inside they're the real rainbow people – and they're magic!"

Mum laughed until she shook all over.
"Do you know, Diandra," Mum said at last,
"I think you're a bit of a magic rainbow person yourself!"

"Good," said Diandra and
she skipped ahead of Mum
all the way home.

OTHER TAMARIND TITLES

A Tamarind Book

Published by Tamarind Ltd, 1999

ISBN 1 870516 44 3

Designed and typeset by Judith Gordon
Printed in Singapore